DIAMOND
Double Play

BY JAKE MADDOX

Text by Shawn Pryor
Illustrated by Sean Tiffany

STONE ARCH BOOKS
a capstone imprint

Jake Maddox Sports Stories is published by
Stone Arch Books
A Capstone Imprint
1710 Roe Crest Drive
North Mankato, Minnesota 56003
www.capstonepub.com

Library of Congress Cataloging-in-Publication Data
Names: Maddox, Jake, author. | Pryor, Shawn, author. | Tiffany, Sean,
    illustrator. | Maddox, Jake. Impact books. Jake Maddox sports story.
Title: Diamond double play / by Jake Maddox and Shawn Pryor ;
    illustrated by Sean Tiffany.
Description: North Mankato, Minnesota : an imprint of Stone Arch Books,
    [2019] | Series: Jake Maddox. Jake Maddox sports stories | Summary:
    Blake Easton has never played organized sports, so when he makes the
    local traveling baseball team as a bench player, he is thrilled; and when
    the team's star second baseman (and all-around annoyance) Kyle, breaks
    his foot in the very first game, the coach calls on Blake to fill in—but
    Blake is not sure he can perform as well as Kyle, and even less sure that
    he can trust Kyle's helpful advice.
Identifiers: LCCN 2019000270| ISBN 9781496583291 (hardcover) |
    ISBN 9781496584526 (pbk.)
Subjects: LCSH: Baseball stories. | Teamwork (Sports)—Juvenile fiction. |
    Self-confidence—Juvenile fiction. | CYAC: Baseball—Fiction. | Teamwork
    (Sports)—Fiction. | Self-confidence—Fiction.
Classification: LCC PZ7.1.P7855 Di 2019 | DDC 813.6 [Fic]—dc23
LC record available at https://lccn.loc.gov/2019000270

Designer: Tracy McCabe

Printed and bound in the USA
PA70

TABLE OF CONTENTS

CHAPTER 1

PLAYGROUND DREAMS

Blake Easton was up to bat. He surveyed the infield, trying to find the right spot to advance the runner on third base and give his team the win.

"Let's go, Blake! You got this!" Franklin, Blake's best friend, yelled from where he waited on third base.

Blake grinned, then made eye contact with the pitcher, his other friend, Taylor. "I'm going to make it easy on you!" Blake shouted. "I'll tell you exactly where the ball is going. I'm going to squeeze it right past second base, so you might want to shift your infield."

"You can't scare me," Taylor retorted from the pitcher's mound. He turned to the infield. "We've got him this time. Last out is at bat!"

Taylor signaled the catcher and wound up the pitch. Then he threw the ball over the plate as hard as he could.

Blake shifted his batting stance and swung. *BOP!*

Just as he'd predicted, the Wiffle ball blazed past second base. It soared into the outfield as Franklin raced home to score the winning run!

"That's the game, guys!" Blake shouted.

Both teams shook hands. All the players congratulated each other after a well-played game at the park.

"You called it!" Franklin exclaimed, giving Blake a high five.

"Eh, I think he just got lucky," Taylor teased, giving Blake a playful shoulder punch. "I'll get him next time. I should've given him my Wiffle curveball. Nobody can touch that one!"

"Maybe. We'll see next weekend," Blake said with a smile. "Hey, the Summit Ice Cream Shop has a two-for-one special. Who's in?"

Shouts of "Me!" rang across the diamond. Everyone grabbed their gear and started making their way out of the park.

As they headed toward the exit, Franklin noticed a flyer taped to the park community board. He wandered over to see what it was.

"Whoa! The Jefferson Mega-Middies—that traveling baseball team—are holding open tryouts!" Franklin announced. The other players quickly gathered around.

"Can anyone try out?" Blake asked.

"It says they're looking for players from eleven to twelve years old," Franklin replied. "Little League experience not necessary, but recommended."

Blake stared at the flyer. *Should I go to the tryouts?* he wondered.

As much as he enjoyed playing Wiffle ball with his friends, his dream was to play in a baseball league—someplace where the games actually counted.

Blake quickly snapped back to reality as Taylor looked directly at him.

"Dude, you should totally try out for this!" Taylor said. He seemed to read Blake's mind. "You don't have to play in Little League to try out. You'd be awesome."

All of Blake's friends knew how much he wanted to play organized baseball. But he'd never told them what held him back.

What if the other players just see me as a backyard athlete? he worried. *What if they don't take me seriously?*

Blake shuffled his feet and sighed. "I don't know . . ." he said. "Yeah, it's open tryouts, but I'm sure the only ones who actually make the team will be all-stars or other Little Leaguers."

"You don't know that for sure," Taylor argued.

"I just play Wiffle ball," Blake said. "I probably wouldn't stand a chance."

"Are you kidding? You're the best hitter and base runner here!" Franklin exclaimed. "And I see you fielding baseballs that you throw against your house all the time. Not to mention practicing your swing with that portable training station your parents got you for your birthday."

"I don't know . . . ," Blake said again.

"Come on, man," Franklin said. "It can't hurt to try out."

"But what if I don't make it?" Blake muttered.

"You'll never know unless you try," Taylor said. "If you make it, we'll be there cheering you on. If you don't, you've always got a spot on Wiffle Saturdays."

Blake stared at the flyer again. He turned to look at his friends, then turned back to look at the flyer. Taking a deep breath, he said, "All right, I'll give it a shot. Now, let's go get some ice cream!"

CHAPTER 2

ENTER THE MEGA-PLEX

The following weekend, Blake hopped out of his parents' car and raced toward the Jefferson Baseball Mega-Plex. His heart was thumping. It was the first day of Mega-Middies tryouts.

Blake had spent practically the whole week practicing in his backyard, trying to keep his nerves from getting the best of him ahead of tryouts. It hadn't entirely worked.

Still anxious, he'd made sure to arrive early today. He wanted to have enough time to warm up and prepare for what was to come.

"Blake! Don't forget your glove!" his dad yelled from the car window.

Blake ran back to get his glove. "Thanks, Dad," he said. "It'd be hard to play without that. I think I have everything else in my bag, so I should be set. I'll text you when tryouts are done."

"Good luck and have fun," his dad said with a smile.

Blake gave his dad a nervous smile, then sprinted toward the Mega-Plex. "This is the real thing," he muttered to himself as he entered the building.

The sounds of baseballs smacking against leather gloves and the tapping of cleats echoed. Blake began to look for Diamond Two, where the Mega-Middies tryouts would take place.

After finding the correct field, Blake sat on the metal bleachers, pulled his cleats out of his bag, and started lacing them up. He glanced around to see what kind of competition he would be up against.

As expected, there were lots of kids he didn't recognize. *They're probably from the local Little League,* Blake thought. But he was relieved to also recognize some classmates from school who, like him, had never played any organized sports.

At least I won't be the only newbie on the field today, thought Blake.

Blake finished tying his shoes, took a deep breath, and whispered, "I've got this." Ready to warm up, he placed his bat bag with the others and grabbed his glove and a ball.

Now he just had to find someone to warm up with. Thankfully he didn't have to look far.

"Hey, are you here for the Mega-Middies tryouts?" a kid asked. "Need to warm up?"

"Yeah and yeah," Blake said, tossing the ball. "I'm Blake. Blake Easton."

"Austin Tavares," the boy replied. "What league do you play in? I've never seen you before." He tossed the ball back to Blake.

"I've never played in any league," Blake admitted. "I mostly just play with my friends. But I've been wanting to play organized baseball for a long time. I figured I'd give it a shot. Hopefully I won't embarrass myself."

Blake threw the ball to Austin, still warming up his arm. "How about you? What league do you play in?" he asked.

"Usually the city league," Austin replied, tossing the ball back. "I've been on the Mega-Middies for the past two years as a bench player, though. Hopefully I get to start this time around."

"Oh," Blake said. Hearing that, his nerves kicked into high gear. Austin had way more experience than he did.

"You'll do fine," Austin assured him. "If you have questions, ask me. We're all here to bring out the best in each other and help one another. Better teammates make for a better team." He smiled.

"Thanks," Blake replied. He smiled gratefully, feeling better about his decision to try out.

Just then an older man who Blake assumed was the coach appeared. He blew his whistle to signal everyone to bring it in.

Austin threw Blake one final warm-up toss. "If you can make it through today's tryouts, you've got a good shot to make the team," he said. "But Coach Sweatt can be tough. It's not going to be easy."

CHAPTER 3

LET THE TRYOUTS BEGIN

Coach Sweatt's whistle echoed. "Circle up, boys!" he shouted.

The hopeful Mega-Middies recruits huddled up.

"I'm glad to see so many eager faces here today," the coach began. "But here's the deal: there are thirty-five of you and only fifteen roster spots. If you want to make this team, you gotta have heart, hustle, determination, and proper conditioning. Let's get started!"

The players cheered as Coach Sweatt blew his whistle again.

"Let's run some laps!" Coach shouted. "Everyone line up at home plate. When I blow the whistle, run the perimeter of the entire field until I tell you to stop!"

Blake and Austin gathered with the others at home plate.

"This is where Coach finds out who's serious about being a part of the team. Just keep a steady pace with me, OK?" Austin said as they tapped gloves.

"OK." Blake nodded.

Just then one of the other players in the huddle walked over. "You out here trying to help the newbies?" the boy said to Austin. He looked over at Blake and sneered. "I've seen you at the park playing Wiffle ball. You might be a backyard all-star, but you don't stand a chance here. Especially not with me around."

"Whatever, Kyle," Austin scoffed. "Maybe you should just worry about not having another 'leg cramp' during conditioning drills like last year." Austin made air quotes when he said "leg cramp."

"Maybe *you* should worry about eating my dust!" Kyle sneered, walking away.

"He seems pleasant," Blake said sarcastically.

Austin rolled his eyes. "That's Kyle. His dad's the third-base coach, so he thinks he can do whatever he wants," he said. "He's a good player, but he's annoying."

PHWEEEEEEEET!

"Let's go, get those laps in! Go!" Coach Sweatt yelled.

The players started running. Blake kept pace with Austin as they ran past first base, around the outfield, and down the third-base line with the others.

After the third lap, some kids started slowing down. After the fifth lap, a few staggered off the field in defeat. After the eighth lap, two more quit. Blake continued to run next to Austin.

After the tenth lap, Coach Sweatt let out another *PHWEEEEEEEET!* from his whistle. "All right, that's enough!" he called. "Bring it in."

The remaining players jogged slowly in and caught their breath. Coach did a quick head count.

"Started with thirty-five, and now we're down to twenty-five. Making this team isn't easy. Go take a water break, and then we'll start with infield and outfield drills," Coach said.

After their break, the remaining players were separated into groups. One coach took the pitchers, another took the outfielders, and Coach Sweatt was left with the infielders—including Austin, Blake, and Kyle.

"Austin to shortstop, Kyle to third, Tracy to first," Coach said. "You, what's your name?" He pointed straight at Blake.

Blake tried to look—and sound—confident. "Blake Easton, Coach."

"Can you play second, Blake?" the coach asked.

"I'll play anywhere, Coach," Blake replied. "I just want a chance to play."

Coach Sweatt smiled. "I like your attitude, kid. Take second."

"Hey!" Kyle exclaimed. "That's my position! Why are you putting him there, Coach? I bet he doesn't even know the position!" Kyle glared at Blake.

"Worry about playing third, Kyle. You'll get your chance," Coach Sweatt said sternly.

Without waiting for a reply, Coach headed for home plate. The players all hurried to their assigned positions.

Coach Sweatt picked up a bat in one hand and a ball in the other. "OK, we've got a runner at first and no outs. Here we go!" he shouted.

Crack!

The ball whizzed toward second base. Blake quickly snatched it in his glove and tossed it to Austin. Austin winged it to first to turn it into a double play.

"Nice play!" Austin yelled as he and Blake tapped gloves.

"He got lucky," grumbled Kyle, just loudly enough for Blake to hear.

Coach grabbed another ball, ready to hit it to the infield again. *Crack!*

This time the ball bounced off the pitcher's mound. Austin misjudged it, and the ball flew by, but Blake was there as backup. He snagged the ball before it left the infield.

"Way to back up your teammate, Blake! That's how you look out for each other on the field!" Coach Sweatt hollered.

Blake grinned, feeling glad that he'd made the decision to try out. Maybe he'd make the Mega-Middies after all.

CHAPTER 4

SWING, BATTER, SWING!

After a brutal first day of tryouts, only eighteen hopeful players remained, including Blake. Knowing Austin had his back had made it easier for Blake to keep up with the rest of the players and handle the defensive and base-running drills.

When he got home that afternoon, Blake texted Franklin and his Wiffle ball friends to let them know he'd survived day one. They were all excited for him, but Blake wasn't quite ready to celebrate. He wasn't a lock to make the team just yet.

It was now day two, and the coaches wanted to see all the players bat before tryouts came to a close.

In the dugout, Blake grabbed his bat. Austin pulled him to the side. "This pitcher has a great curveball," he said. "Be patient, and wait for the ball to break."

Blake nodded. "Thanks," he said.

"Blake, you're up!" Coach Sweatt called.

Blake adjusted his batting gloves as he walked to the batter's box. He got into a proper batting stance, surveyed the field, and looked back at the pitcher. These next at-bats could make or break his chance at becoming one of the Mega-Middies.

From second base, Kyle yelled, "Hey, the newbie is up! Infield in! There's no way he can hit Ramon. He's our best pitcher!"

Blake gripped his bat and awaited the pitch. *I can do this,* he told himself. *It's just like Wiffle ball—except a lot more pressure.*

Ramon began his windup. Blake's eyes widened as the fastball sped toward him.

Crack! he swung and connected. The ball shot over the third baseman's head and bounced into the outfield for a blooper single.

"Not bad, but let's switch it up a bit," Coach Sweatt said. He signaled to Ramon for a different pitch.

Blake waited in the batter's box, ready to swing. Ramon threw another pitch. It was the curveball Austin had warned him about. Blake completely whiffed on the pitch.

"See, I told you he's just a backyard superstar!" Kyle jeered. "Give him that pitch again, Ramon. He can't hit it!"

Ramon threw another curveball. Blake was late swinging but connected for a foul ball.

"Remember what I told you!" Austin shouted from the dugout.

Blake nodded and waited for the pitch. Another curveball, directly in the strike zone.

This time Blake kept his eye on the ball. He knew where the pitch was going to break and squared up the bat, making direct contact with the ball.

Crack-kow! The ball blazed down the first-base line, sending a mean line drive down the field!

"Well done, Blake!" Coach Sweatt said, smiling. "All right, let's call it a day. All of you hustled hard and did great today. I wish we could keep all of you, but unfortunately that's not possible. I'll be calling you tomorrow to let you know if you've made the team. Thanks for your hard work, and good luck!"

CHAPTER 5

THE CALL

The following afternoon, Blake paced nervously back and forth across his living room. He still hadn't heard a word from Coach Sweatt, and it was almost the end of the day.

"Keep it up and you're going to wear ruts in the carpet," Blake's dad said.

Blake paused. "Sorry, Dad," he said. "I'm just nervous about this call from Coach. I want to make the team so badly. I'm scared it's not going to happen."

Blake's mom smiled. "If you gave it your all and did your best, then that's all you can do," she told him. "No matter what happens, we're proud of you."

Dad handed Blake his baseball glove. "Why don't the two of you go outside and toss the ball a little bit?" he suggested. "I'll let you know if Coach calls."

Mom pulled her glove out from the closet. "That's a good idea," she agreed.

For the next twenty minutes, Blake and his mom tossed the ball back and forth. After a particularly hard throw, Blake paused.

"Too much heat for ya?" his mom asked, laughing.

"You're just trying to break the webbing in my glove." Blake chuckled. "Thanks for coming out here to throw with me. I needed the distraction."

Just then, the screen door creaked loudly. Blake and his mom both turned toward the porch.

"Son, Coach Sweatt is on the phone for you!" Dad hollered.

Blake raced inside, almost knocking his dad over in his hurry. "Hey, Coach!" he said, picking up the phone.

"Good evening, Blake. How are you doing?" asked Coach Sweatt.

Blake's nerves were starting to get the best of him. *What if he's calling to say I didn't make the team?* he worried. But he tried to play it cool. "I'm OK," he replied.

"Good. Listen, I have to say, I was really impressed with the way you carried yourself during tryouts," Coach Sweatt continued. "It's rare to see a kid with zero league experience hold his own with all-stars and city leaguers."

"Thanks!" Blake exclaimed. Coach's praise had to be a good sign, right? "I had a blast."

"I'm going to cut to the chase," Coach said. "You made the team. You've got the hustle and heart I like to see in my players. Welcome to the Mega-Middies."

"I made the team?" Blake practically shouted.

He wanted to scream with joy, but he didn't want to embarrass himself on the phone.

"I mean, thanks, Coach!" Blake said. "Thanks for giving me a chance!"

"No problem, Blake," said Coach Sweatt. "Our first official practice will be tomorrow evening at the Mega-Plex. We'll practice three days a week. Games are on the weekends, and our first game is in two weeks. We'll have a twenty-game season, and if we win at least ten games, we qualify for the state tournament."

"That sounds awesome, Coach!" Blake said. He smiled as he took in all the details. "What position am I playing?"

He didn't want to get his hopes up, but Blake couldn't help but wonder, *Do I have a chance to start?*

Coach Sweatt paused. "You'll be backing up Kyle at second base to start," he said. "You definitely have skills, but they're still raw. You need time to practice. We'll get you in the game when we can, but don't expect to play too much."

Blake's heart sank. He knew it had been a long shot, but he was still disappointed not to be a starter. *Still,* he reminded himself, *I did make the team. I wasn't even sure* that *was possible.*

Blake picked himself up and replied, "OK, Coach, that works for me. Thanks again for giving me a shot."

"See you tomorrow at seven o'clock. Be ready to play!" Coach Sweatt said before hanging up the phone.

Blake ran back outside, almost tearing the screen door off its hinges. "I made the team! I made the team!" he shouted. "I can't believe it! I'm going to be on the Mega-Middies!"

* * *

The next day, the players who'd made the team gathered back at the Mega-Plex. The assistant coaches handed out jerseys and game schedules to all the Mega-Middies.

Coach Sweatt picked up his clipboard. "OK, you should all know your own positions, but here's our lineup: Ramon, Phillip, and Michael, you're pitching. Jermaine will start in left field, Victor will start in center field, and Billy will be in right field."

Coach continued down the list. "Our starting infield has Corey at third, Austin at shortstop, Kyle at second, Tracy at first, and Jason catching," he announced. "And our bench will consist of Blake, Mario, Kelly, and Randall."

Blake let out a disappointed sigh. He knew he wasn't a starter, but hearing he was on the bench still stung a little.

Seeming to sense his friend's disappointment, Austin turned to Blake. "Hey, I didn't start my first two years on the Mega-Middies," he said. "This is my first year starting, so don't beat yourself up. You're still a part of this team."

Blake nodded. Austin had a point. "Thanks, man," he said. "You're right. I might not be a starter, but I'll make the best of it when I get the chance."

CHAPTER 6

A TRAGIC TURN

During their season opener against the Koss City Stallions, Blake cheered on his teammates from the dugout. At the bottom of the sixth inning, they were holding on to a 1–0 lead.

With one out and a runner on first, the Jefferson Mega-Middies waited for Ramon to deliver the pitch to the Stallions player at the plate. Ramon wound up and threw a monster fastball.

CRACK! The ball sped toward the right side of second base. Kyle stretched to grab the ground ball as the Stallions player on first took off running.

Austin sped to second base. He held up his glove for Kyle to throw him the ball.

But Kyle seemed to want to do it all on his own. He rushed to beat the runner to second base, getting his foot on the base seconds before the opposing player. Then he turned to make the throw to first, hoping to turn it into a double play.

But even from the bench, Blake could see that Kyle's foot had hit second base at a weird angle. As he made the throw to first, Kyle cried out in pain.

"OUT!" the umpire bellowed as the first baseman caught the ball. "That's the ballgame!"

The Mega-Middies coaches hurried over to Kyle, who was on the ground, clutching his cleat. Blake and the rest of the players trailed after them.

"My foot! I can't put any weight on it! It hurts, it hurts!" Kyle shouted, pounding his fist in the dirt.

"It's OK," Coach Harris, Kyle's dad, said. "We'll get you to the emergency room."

Coach Harris and Coach Sweatt carried Kyle off the field as the rest of the team looked on solemnly. The players and parents from the opposing team clapped as a sign of support. Moments later, Kyle's father drove him to the hospital.

Next to Blake, Austin shuddered. "That looked really bad. I shouted for him to throw me the ball. I don't know why he didn't listen. We could've turned the double play *and* he wouldn't be hurt."

"You know how Kyle is," said Ramon, shaking his head. "He never learns."

Coach Sweatt returned to the field. "Well, you boys played a tough game today. I'm sure we're all happy to have won, but I know I speak for everyone when I say I'm sad at how it ended. Hopefully, Kyle will be OK. I'll let you know what I hear tomorrow. Bring it in."

The team huddled in close and shouted, "MEGA-MIDDIES!" then trotted off the field.

"Hey, Blake," Coach Sweatt said. "Can I talk to you for a moment?"

Blake turned as the other players headed toward the dugout to get their equipment. "Sure, Coach. What's up?" he asked.

"Between you and me, Kyle's ankle didn't look good," Coach said. "Depending on what the doctor says, I want you ready to take his place at second."

Blake nodded, not knowing what to say. *There's a reason I was on the bench. I'm not ready to start!* he thought. *What if I make a mistake? What if Coach puts me back on the bench for the rest of the season?*

Blake's anxiety began to build. He'd wanted to be a starter, but not like this.

CHAPTER 7

FROM THE BENCH TO THE FIELD

The next day, the Mega-Middies sat in the dugout. They were all waiting for their next practice to begin. "Has anybody seen Kyle?" Blake asked.

Before anyone could answer, Coach Sweatt stepped into the dugout. "I've got some good news," he said. He stepped away from the dugout opening as Kyle walked in.

The team cheered and surrounded their injured teammate. It took a minute for Blake to register that Kyle was wearing an Aircast boot.

"The doctor said I have a broken foot. I'll be in this boot for most of the season," Kyle said. "But the good news is I still get to travel with the team, even though I can't play."

"Blake, with Kyle out, you're in at second base," Coach said. "OK, guys, on the field."

Before Blake could leave the dugout, Kyle pulled him aside. "Hey, listen," he said. "I know I've given you a hard time since you first got here and . . . I'm sorry."

Blake could feel the shock on his face. Kyle must have seen it too.

"I know you might not believe me," he said, "but my dad gave me a pretty good lecture at the hospital yesterday. He made me realize I haven't been a very good teammate. I only have myself to blame for trying to show off. I mean, look where it got me." He motioned to his Aircast. "Don't be dumb like I was. Play smart out there."

Blake hesitated. *Can I really trust Kyle?* he wondered. But truthfully, he didn't have much choice.

"Thanks, man," Blake finally said.

The boys bumped fists. Then Blake ran out onto the diamond, ready to play second base.

"Let's turn some double plays!" Coach Sweatt called. He hit the ball toward Corey at third base.

As Corey scooped up the ball, Blake hurried to cover second. He caught the throw from third and scrambled to get the ball to first. It wasn't his best throw, but the ball made it there.

Before Coach Sweatt could hit the ball again, Kyle interrupted from the dugout. "Coach!" he shouted. "I think I see something that might help Blake."

"All right, Kyle. What do you see?" Coach Sweatt asked.

Kyle stood up and made his way toward the field. "OK. Blake, you did a good job turning the double play, but you're standing too close to the first baseman. You're having to run farther to turn the play."

"Really? Where should I be, then?" asked Blake.

"Take three steps to the right," replied Kyle. "Only shift toward first if the coach signals the infield to shift left."

Blake got into the proper position on the field. "Gotcha," he said. "Coach, can we run the play again?" He wanted to see if Kyle's suggestion would make a difference.

Coach Sweatt nodded and hit the ball again. This time, Blake didn't feel as rushed. He made a perfect throw to Tracy at first base.

"Nice play, guys!" Austin called.

"That was a lot easier. Thanks for backing me up, Kyle!" Blake said.

"No problem," Kyle said with a smile. "It's what teammates do."

CHAPTER 8

GAME TIME

As the Mega-Middies took the field to play their next game, against the Gate City Eagles, butterflies swirled in Blake's stomach. He'd only had two practices with the team as their starting second baseman. They'd gone fairly well, but playing in an actual game was a lot of pressure.

Blake had talked to Franklin the night before, hoping to ease his nerves, but it had backfired. Franklin had announced that he and the rest of the Wiffle ball players were planning to be at the game, cheering on Blake.

Great, Blake had thought. *Even more people to bear witness if I blow it.*

Now he took a deep breath, exhaled, and got into his proper position on the field.

"You ready?" Austin asked. He looked over at Blake from his spot at shortstop.

"Yeah," Blake replied. He began to sweat as the game started. He wished it was from the heat of the sun, not his nerves.

Phillip, the Mega-Middies backup pitcher, was on the mound to start. The Eagles batter swung at the first pitch and hit a line drive to right field. He rounded first base and jogged back to the bag.

The next Eagles batter took the first pitch as well. He hit a foul ball that was within reach of the catcher.

"OUT!" yelled the umpire.

"One down!" Austin hollered to his teammates.

"Try to turn two, guys!" Coach Sweatt yelled from the dugout.

The next batter got into a long battle with Phillip. No matter which pitch was thrown, the batter kept hitting foul ball after foul ball, wearing Phillip down.

Finally the batter hit a line drive straight toward Blake. Before he could get his glove down, the ball bounced off his cleat. By the time Blake was finally able to regain control, the lead runner had made it to third base. Thankfully the batter only made it to first.

Blake shook his head in disappointment. He'd already made one error. The last thing he wanted to do in his first-ever start was blow the game for his team and embarrass himself in front of his friends.

"Hey! Don't you put your head down, shake it off! You got this, Blake!" Kyle shouted from the dugout.

"We all make mistakes! Move on from it and get ready for the next play!" Coach Sweatt shouted.

Blake looked over and shook his head. As upset as he was, Kyle and Coach Sweatt were right. He'd only be letting his team down if he gave up. He had to focus.

Blake got back into position, smacked his glove with his hand, and waited for the clean-up hitter to swing.

"Hit it at the second baseman!" one of the Eagles players shouted. "He's scared!"

"Yeah, keep the pressure on him, and we'll get easy runs all day!" another Eagles player jeered.

Blake tried his best to block out the insults, watching as the batter swung. The batter hit a sizzling ground ball right toward Blake!

This time Blake stayed focused and on his toes. He got in front of the ball, put his glove on the ground, and scooped it. He whirled and tossed it to Austin, turning a fantastic double play and preventing the Eagles from scoring.

"That's how you shake it off!" Austin cheered. He tapped gloves with Blake as the Mega-Middies ran to the dugout.

Blake exhaled. He was glad they'd been able to get out of that jam, but he knew the game was far from over.

CHAPTER 9

LOOK FOR THE SIGN

At the bottom of the fifth inning, the Mega-Middies trailed 2–1. Austin was up to bat, and Blake was on deck.

Blake watched closely, waiting for his chance to help his team. He had grounded out during his first at-bat and struck out during his second.

This is my last chance to prove myself, he thought.

Austin waited patiently for his pitch. After four consecutive balls from the Eagles pitcher, Austin drew a walk and jogged to first base.

Blake took a couple more practice swings, then headed to the batter's box. His teammates cheered him on as he planted his feet, crouched in his batting stance, and waited for his pitch.

The Eagles pitcher wound up and delivered the first pitch. Blake took a massive swing and missed.

"Strike!" the umpire hollered.

Blake looked at Coach Sweatt, who signaled with his hands for Blake to calm down. "Wait for your pitch!" Coach called from his position near first base.

Raising his hand toward the umpire, Blake signaled for a time-out. He adjusted his footing in the batter's box, then motioned that he was ready. The umpire signaled for the game to continue.

"You've got this!" Franklin yelled from the stands. Blake's other Wiffle ball friends also hollered out their encouragement.

The Eagles pitcher wound up and delivered a changeup that didn't clear the plate. Blake stayed patient and didn't swing.

"Ball!" called out the umpire.

Blake tightened up his grip on the bat, waiting for the next pitch to come his way. The pitcher stepped into his delivery as Austin edged off first base.

Crack!

Blake connected and sent the ball over the third baseman's head. Blake raced to first base, and Austin advanced to second. The Mega-Middies cheered. They had two players on base with no outs.

"Nice hit!" said Coach Sweatt, giving Blake a high five. "Now, stay ready."

Blake nodded at Coach Sweatt as Victor, their center fielder, came up to the plate. Then he turned his attention to the third-base coach, who was relaying signals to both Austin and Blake.

Blake understood the signal, as did Austin. They were going for the steal. Both boys began to edge off their respective bases.

The pitcher sensed what was happening and turned to throw out Blake at first. Blake quickly slid back to the base, avoiding the tag. Then he got up from the ground, dusted himself off, and checked with the base coach. The signal hadn't changed.

Back at home plate, Victor didn't make contact with the first two pitches. As the pitcher got ready to throw again, Blake and Austin slowly edged off their bases. Then they took off and attempted a double steal!

"Strike! You're out!" the umpire yelled to Victor.

The catcher tried to throw out Blake as he was stealing second, but the throw was too late.

"Yeah!" Blake cheered. He and Austin had managed to pull off the double steal. Scanning the crowd, he could see his Wiffle ball buddies in the stands, cheering him on.

With the tying run on third and a leading run on second, it was Jermaine's turn at bat.

"Come on, Jermaine! Bring us home!" Blake yelled.

Jermaine swung at the first pitch, popping up to the first baseman. Blake sighed. With two outs, the Mega-Middies' chance of a win began to look slim.

Corey was next to bat. He had already walked twice today and had been itching to get a hit. The pitcher wound up and threw a fastball straight down the middle.

Corey's eyes lit up like a firecracker as he pulled a line drive down the first-base line. Blake took off running, and Austin raced home. He crossed the plate, bringing the score to 2–2.

But the Mega-Middies didn't stop there. As the right fielder picked up the ball, the third-base coach signaled Blake to run home.

The right fielder's throw toward home plate was right on target. Blake ran with all his might. He slid into home just as the catcher swung his glove down to tag Blake.

As the dust cleared, the umpire yelled, "SAFE!"

The Mega-Middies celebrated in the dugout as they took a 3–2 lead! Blake dusted himself off as his teammates patted him on the back.

"Not bad for a newbie!" Kyle said.

CHAPTER 10

DOWN TO THE WIRE

As the Eagles prepared for their final at-bats, the Mega-Middies took the field.

"This is the toughest part of their lineup," Austin said to his teammates. "Stay alert and back each other up. We can do this!"

Phillip finished his final warm-up pitch as the Eagles catcher, who was three-for-three with two doubles, came up to bat. After throwing a strike, Phillip threw four consecutive balls, sending the Eagles player to first base.

The next Eagles batter stepped up to bat. *Pop!* A pop fly soared into the air on the left side of the infield. Both Blake and Tracy started chasing it.

"I've got it! It's closer to me!" Tracy called.

Blake stepped back, letting Tracy catch the ball. There was no sense in competing with his teammate over an easy out. Tracy caught the ball and tossed it to the pitcher.

"One out with a runner on first!" Blake called, getting back into position. "Let's go!"

The next batter stepped up to the plate.

"Hey, he's the fastest one on their team! If we can't pull the double play, make sure we get the force out at second!" Austin warned his teammates.

Austin was right. The batter at the plate had already stolen two bases and scored both the Eagles' runs that day.

Phillip wound up and delivered the pitch.

"Foul ball!" the umpire roared.

The next pitch came. "Ball!" the umpire called.

Feeling the pressure, Phillip breathed deeply and threw another pitch.

"Ball!" the umpire said, yet again.

Getting frustrated, Phillip did his best to focus and deliver a solid pitch.

The Eagles batter hit a grounder to Austin, who tossed it to Blake at second base for the out. But before Blake could even attempt the double play at first, the super-fast Eagles player was there.

Austin alerted his teammates again: "Two down! Man on first! We can get the force at second or take it to first, whatever's easiest. Let's go, Middies!"

The Mega-Middies got down into their positions as the next Eagles player came to the plate.

Phillip threw the pitch, and *pow!* The batter crushed the ball down the right-field line.

The speedy lead runner for the Eagles rounded second. Blake ran toward the outfield to get the relay throw from the right fielder.

As Blake caught the ball, he heard his teammates screaming for him to throw it home. He turned and saw the lead runner sprinting around third.

This is it, Blake thought. He focused and threw the ball as hard as he could to home plate. It arrived just as the runner slid home.

"You're out!" the umpire shouted. "That's the game!"

The Mega-Middies had won! Blake's teammates shouted and jumped as they surrounded him.

"That was one heck of a throw!" Austin cheered.

"Where did you learn to make a play like that?" Kyle asked, grinning.

"From the backyard all-star league!" Blake said with a laugh. "And I've learned even more being a part of this team. Luckily, it just all came together at the right time."

AUTHOR BIO

Shawn Pryor is the creator and co-writer of the all-ages graphic novel mystery series Cash & Carrie, writer of *Kentucky Kaiju*, and writer and co-creator of the football/drama series *Force*. He is one of the co-founders of Action Lab Entertainment and currently serves as their president of creative relations. Find out more about his works at www.shawnpryor.com.

ILLUSTRATOR BIO

Sean Tiffany has worked in the illustration and comic book field for more than twenty years. He has illustrated more than sixty children's books for Capstone and has been an instructor at the famed Joe Kubert School in northern New Jersey. Raised on a small island off the coast of Maine, Sean now resides in Boulder, Colorado, with his wife, Monika, their son, James, a cactus named Jim, and a room full of entirely too many guitars.

GLOSSARY

anxious (ANGK-shuhs)—afraid or nervous about what may happen

conditioning (kuhn-DISH-uh-ning)—the process of becoming stronger and healthier by following a regular exercise program and diet

league (LEEG)—an association of people or groups with common interests or goals

lineup (LINE-uhp)—a list of players taking part in a game

organized (OR-guh-nized)—arranged into a formal group with leaders and with rules for doing or planning things

position (puh-ZISH-uhn)—the place where a person or thing is or should be

pressure (PRESH-er)—a force or influence that cannot be avoided

recruits (ri-KROOTS)—newcomers to a group or field of activity

respective (ri-SPEK-tiv)—not the same or shared

roster (ROS-ter)—an orderly list of people belonging to some group

superstar (SOO-per-stahr)—someone who is very talented in a craft, job, entertainment, or sport

tryout (TRYE-out)—a test of the ability, such as with an athlete or an actor, to fill a part or meet standards

DISCUSSION QUESTIONS

1. Why was Blake hesitant to try out for the Mega-Middies? What do you think was holding him back? Do you think he had a good reason to be nervous?

2. Austin was willing to help Blake during team tryouts. Why? Have you ever played a team sport where another teammate was willing to help a new player? Talk about how that person helped you or someone else.

3. Why was Kyle so upset when Coach Sweatt asked him to play third base during tryouts? Have you ever had to deal with a teammate you didn't get along with? Talk about how you dealt with that person during practices or games.

WRITING PROMPTS

1. When Blake makes the throw at the end of the game to help the Mega-Middies win, the team celebrates in victory. Have you ever had a winning moment like Blake's? Write a paragraph about your experience and how it made you feel.

2. This story is told from Blake's point of view, but there are times it's useful to consider a story from another character's perspective. Try rewriting Chapter 6 from Kyle's point of view.

3. In Chapter 3, Coach Sweatt says his players need heart, hustle, determination, and proper conditioning to make the team. Why do you feel those four things are so important to him? Have you ever had a coach or teacher who had a certain set of expectations? How did that make you feel?

BASEBALL GLOSSARY

ball (BAWL)—a pitch not swung at by the batter that fails to pass through the strike zone

catcher (KACH-er)—a baseball player positioned behind home plate

double play (DUHB-ulh PLAY)—a play in baseball by which two base runners are put out

dugout (DUHG-out)—a low shelter facing a baseball diamond and containing the players' bench

first base (FURST BAYSS)—the base that must be touched first by a base runner; also the position of the player who defends the area around first base

infield (IN-feeld)—the area of a baseball field enclosed by the three bases and home plate; also the defensive positions making up first base, second base, shortstop, and third base, and the players who play these positions

outfield (OUT-feeld)—the part of a baseball field beyond the infield and between the foul lines; also the baseball defensive positions comprising right field, center field, and left field and the players who occupy those positions

pitcher (PICH-er)—the player who throws the ball to the batter in baseball or softball

pop fly (POP FLYE)—a high fly ball into the infield or immediately beyond it that can be easily caught before reaching the ground

second base (SEK-uhnd BAYSS)—the base that must be touched second by a base runner; also the position of the player who defends the area near second base

shortstop (SHORT-stop)—the player position in baseball responsible for defending the infield area on the third-base side of second base

strike (STRIKE)—a pitched ball that is in the strike zone or is swung at and is not hit fair

third base (THURD BAYSS)—the base that must be touched third by a base runner; also the position of the player who defends the area near third base

THE FUN DOESN'T STOP HERE!